HI! FLY GUY

Tedd Arnold

SCHOLASTIC INC.
New York   Toronto   London   Auckland
Sydney   Mexico City   New Delhi   Hong Kong

For Sam and Eli
—T.A.

All rights reserved. Published by Scholastic Inc.
SCHOLASTIC, CARTWHEEL BOOKS, and associated logos
are trademarks and/or registered trademarks of Scholastic Inc.
Library of Congress Cataloging-in-Publication Data:
Arnold, Tedd.
Hi, Fly Guy! / by Tedd Arnold.
p. cm.
"Cartwheel books."
Summary: When Buzz captures a fly to enter in The Amazing Pet Show, his parents
and the judges tell him that a fly cannot be a pet, but Fly Guy proves them wrong.
ISBN 978-0-439-63903-3
[1. Flies—Fiction. 2. Pet shows—Fiction.] I. Title.
PZ7.A7379Hi 2005
[E]—dc22   2004020553
ISBN 978-0-439-63903-3

20 19 18 17 16 15   14

Printed in Singapore 46
First printing, September 2005

Chapter 1

A fly went flying.

He was looking
for something to eat—

something tasty,

something slimy.

A boy went walking.

He was looking for
something to catch—
something smart,
something for
The Amazing Pet Show.

The boy caught the
fly in a jar.
"A pet!" he said.

The fly was mad.
He wanted to be free.
He stomped his foot
and said— **BUZZ!**

The boy was surprised.
He said, "You know my name!
You are the smartest pet in
the world!"

Chapter 2

Buzz took the fly home.

"This is my pet," Buzz said
to Mom and Dad.

"He is smart. He can say
my name. Listen!"

Buzz opened the jar.
The fly flew out.

"Flies can't be pets!" said
Dad. "They are pests!"
He got the fly swatter.
The fly cried— **BUZZ!**

And Buzz came to the rescue.
"You are right," said Dad.
"This fly <u>is</u> smart!"

"He needs a name," said Mom.
Buzz thought for a minute.
"Fly Guy," said Buzz.
And Fly Guy said— BUZZ!

It was time for lunch.
Buzz gave Fly Guy
something to eat.

Fly Guy was happy.

Chapter 3

Buzz took Fly Guy to
The Amazing Pet Show.

The judges laughed.

"Flies can't be pets," they said.

"Flies are pests!"

Buzz was sad.

He opened the jar.

"Shoo, Fly Guy," he said.

"Flies can't be pets."

But Fly Guy liked Buzz.
He had an idea.
He did some fancy flying.

The judges were amazed.
"The fly can do tricks," they said.
"But flies can't be pets."

Then Fly Guy said—

The judges were more amazed. "The fly knows the boy's name," they said. "But flies can't be pets."

Fly Guy flew high, high, high into the sky!

Then he dived down, down,
down into the jar.

"The fly knows his jar!" the judges said. "This fly <u>is</u> a pet!" They let Fly Guy in the show.

He even won an award.

And so began a beautiful
friendship.

SUPER FLY GUY

Tedd Arnold

SCHOLASTIC INC.

New York   Toronto   London   Auckland
Sydney   Mexico City   New Delhi   Hong Kong

For Little Tate William
—T.A.

Library of Congress Cataloging-in-Publication Data:

Arnold, Tedd.
Super Fly Guy / by Tedd Arnold.
p. cm.
"Fly Guy #2."
"Cartwheel Books."
Summary: Fly Guy visits the school cafeteria and gets
the lunch lady fired.
ISBN 978-0-439-63904-0
[1. Flies--Fiction. 2. Schools--Fiction. 3. School lunchrooms, cafeterias,
etc.--Fiction.] I. Title.

PZ7.A7379Sup 2006

[E]--dc22   2005007933

ISBN 978-0-439-63904-0

20 19 18 17 16 15 14 13 12 11   11 12 13 14/0

Printed in Singapore 46
First printing, March 2006

A boy had a pet fly.
The fly was named Fly Guy.
Fly Guy could say the boy's
name—

Chapter 1

One day Fly Guy went
to school with Buzz.

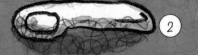

Fly Guy learned about
reading and phonics.

He learned about art.

Then it was lunchtime.
Fly Guy loved the lunchroom.

He loved the dirty dishes.

He loved the smelly mop.

He loved the garbage cans.

Fly Guy met the lunch lady.
Her name was Roz.

"No flies in the
lunchroom!" Roz said.
Fly Guy said—

"This fly is smart," said Roz.
"He knows my name!"

She fed Fly Guy chicken bones
and fish heads in sour milk.
Fly Guy was happy.

Chapter 2

Roz's boss was not happy. "The children cannot eat in a room full of flies!" he said. "You are fired!"

Roz was sad. Fly Guy was sad.
Buzz and the children were sad
because Roz was a good cook.

The next day, Roz was gone. Miss Muzzle was the new lunch lady.

She made burnt peas and
turnips. No one in school
ate lunch—not even Fly Guy,
who ate almost anything.

Everyone missed Roz.
Even the boss missed Roz.

That night, Buzz made a plan.

Chapter 3

The next day, Fly Guy went to school again. In the lunchroom Fly Guy said—

Miss Muzzle looked up.
Fly Guy boinked her on the nose.

BOINK

Miss Muzzle cried, "No flies in my lunchroom!"

She grabbed her swatter
and swung. She missed.

She missed again.

She missed again.

She missed again.

She missed again.

The boss was not happy.
"The children cannot eat
in this mess," he said.
"You are fired!"

The next day, Roz was back.
"You are a super Fly Guy!"

Roz made a special garbage soup for Super Fly Guy.

Fly Guy was happy.

Everyone was happy.

SHOO, FLY GUY!

Tedd Arnold

Cartwheel
B·O·O·K·S ®

SCHOLASTIC INC.
New York   Toronto   London   Auckland
Sydney   Mexico City   New Delhi   Hong Kong

Specially for Zachary Chase
—T. A.

Copyright © 2006 by Tedd Arnold.
Library of Congress Cataloging-in-Publication Data:
Arnold, Tedd.
Shoo, Fly Guy! / Tedd Arnold.
p. cm.
"Cartwheel books."
Summary: A pet fly searches for his favorite brown, oozy, lumpy, smelly food.
ISBN 978-0-439-63905-7
[1. Flies—Fiction.] I. Title.
PZ7.A7379Sh 2006
[E]--dc22   2005028746
ISBN 978-0-439-63905-7

20 19 18 17 16 15 14 13 12 11   11 12 13 14 15
Printed in Singapore 46
First printing, September 2006

Chapter 1

A boy had a pet fly.
The boy called his pet Fly Guy.
Fly Guy could say the boy's
name—

BUZZ!

Buzz played with Fly Guy.

Buzz made him a glass house.

Best of all, Buzz fed him.

Fly Guy's favorite food
was brown, oozy,
lumpy, and smelly.

One day Fly Guy went
flying by himself.

When he came home,
Buzz was gone.

Fly Guy was hungry.
So off he flew.

Chapter 2

Fly Guy flew until he saw something to eat.

It wasn't oozy, lumpy, or smelly. But it was brown. Close enough!

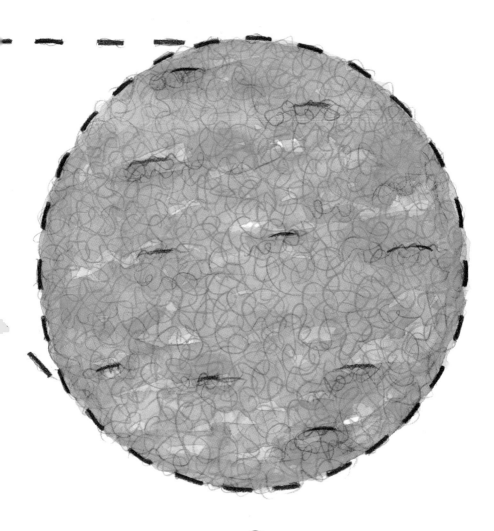

A boy shouted,
"That is my hamburger!"

"Shoo, fly!"

Fly Guy flew on until he
saw something else.

It wasn't brown, lumpy, or smelly. But it was oozy. Close enough!

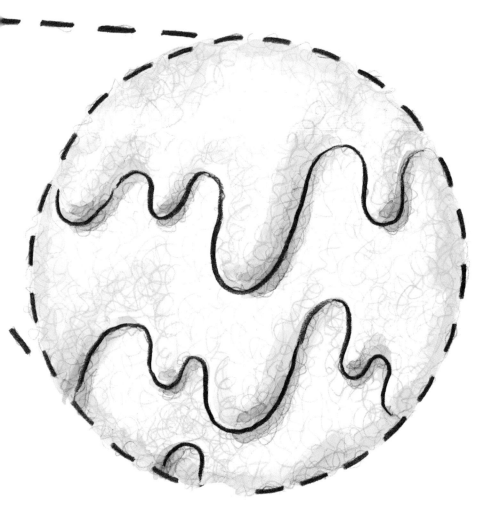

A girl yelled,
"That is my pizza!"

"Shoo, fly!"

Fly Guy flew on until
he saw something else.

It wasn't brown, oozy, or smelly. But it was lumpy. Close enough!

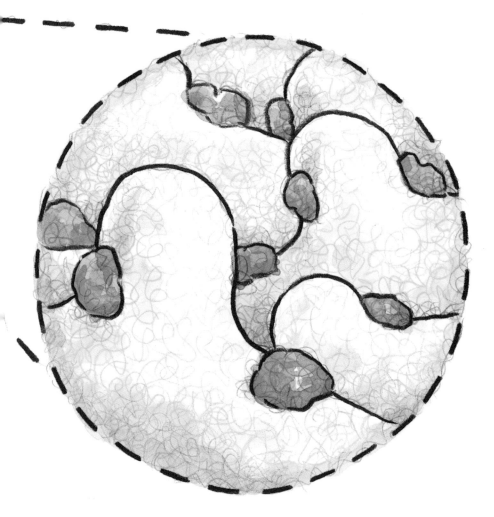

A dog growled,
"Those are my bones."

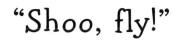

"Shoo, fly!"

Fly Guy flew on until he
saw something else.

It wasn't brown, oozy, or lumpy. But it was smelly. Close enough!

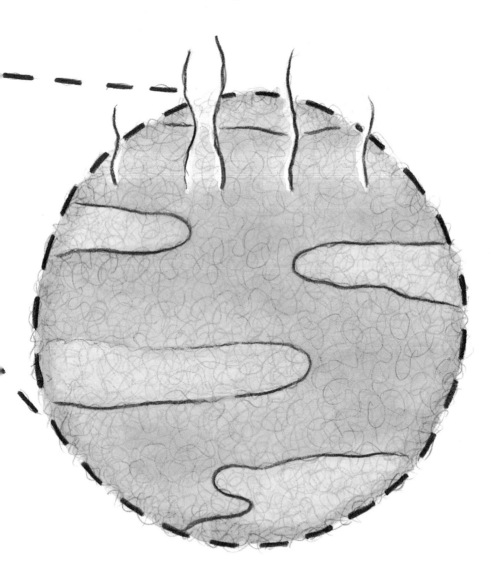

A bird squawked,
"That is my roadkill."

"Shoo, fly!"

Chapter 3

Fly Guy was very hungry.
And he was very tired.
He looked around.
Fly Guy was very lost.

He flew on and on and on and

and on until...

Fly Guy saw something.
Could it be? Yes!

It was brown, oozy,
lumpy, and smelly.

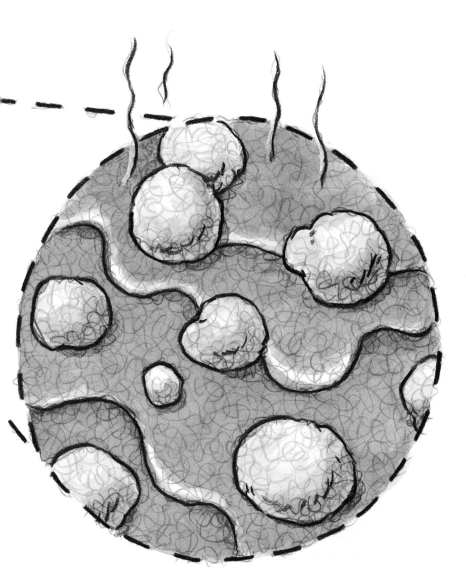

"You found our picnic!"
cried Buzz. "And here is
your favorite—Shoo Fly Pie!"
Fly Guy was very happy!

THERE WAS AN OLD LADY WHO SWALLOWED FLY GUY

Tedd Arnold

Cartwheel
·B·O·O·K·S· ®

SCHOLASTIC INC.
New York   Toronto   London   Auckland
Sydney   Mexico City   New Delhi   Hong Kong

For Marissa, Benjamin, Ethan,
Gary, and Amy — of course!
—T. A.

All rights reserved. Published by Scholastic Inc.
SCHOLASTIC, CARTWHEEL BOOKS, and associated logos
are trademarks and/or registered trademarks of Scholastic Inc.
No part of this publication may be reproduced, stored in a retrieval system, or transmitted
in any form or by any means, electronic, mechanical, photocopying, recording, or otherwise,
without written permission of the publisher. For information regarding permission, write to
Scholastic Inc., Attention: Permissions Department, 557 Broadway, New York, NY 10012.
Library of Congress Cataloging-in-Publication Data
Arnold, Tedd.
There was an old lady who swallowed Fly Guy/ Tedd Arnold.
p. cm.
"Cartwheel books."
Summary: After accidentally swallowing her grandson's pet fly, Grandma
tries to retrieve it by consuming progressively larger animals.
ISBN 978-0-439-63906-4
[1. Flies--Fiction. 2. Pets--Fiction. 3. Grandmothers--Fiction. 4.
Humorous stories.] I. Title.
PZ7 .A7379TH 2007   [E]--DC22
2006037714
ISBN 978-0-439-63906-4

10   11 12 13 14

Printed in Singapore 46
First printing, September 2007

A young boy named Buzz
had a pet fly.
No one knows why
he had a pet fly.
Buzz named him Fly Guy.

Chapter 1

One day Buzz went
to visit his grandma.
Fly Guy went, too.

Grandma was happy
to see Buzz.
She ran to hug him.

"Hi, Grandma!" said Buzz.
"I want you to meet my pet..."

Grandma said—

and she swallowed Fly Guy.

Buzz didn't know why
she swallowed Fly Guy.

Chapter 2

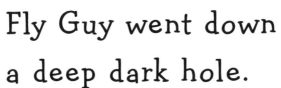

Fly Guy went down
a deep dark hole.

At the bottom of the hole,
he came to a wet place.

He looked around for a while.
Then he wanted to leave.

He started up the hole.

Just then, Grandma
swallowed a spider
to catch Fly Guy.

She swallowed a bird
to catch the spider.

She swallowed a cat
to catch the bird.

She swallowed a dog
to catch the cat.

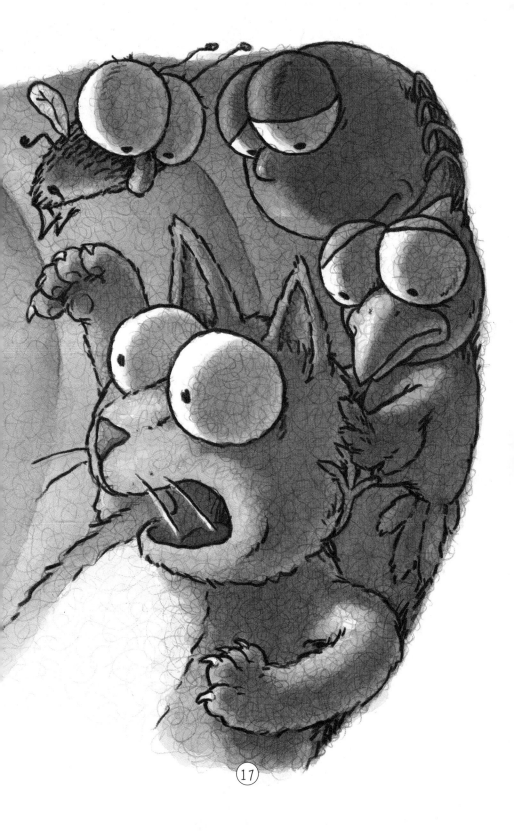

She swallowed a goat
to catch the dog.

She swallowed a cow
to catch the goat.

20

Chapter 3

Grandma was about to
swallow a horse
to catch the cow.

Fly Guy cried, **BUZZ!**

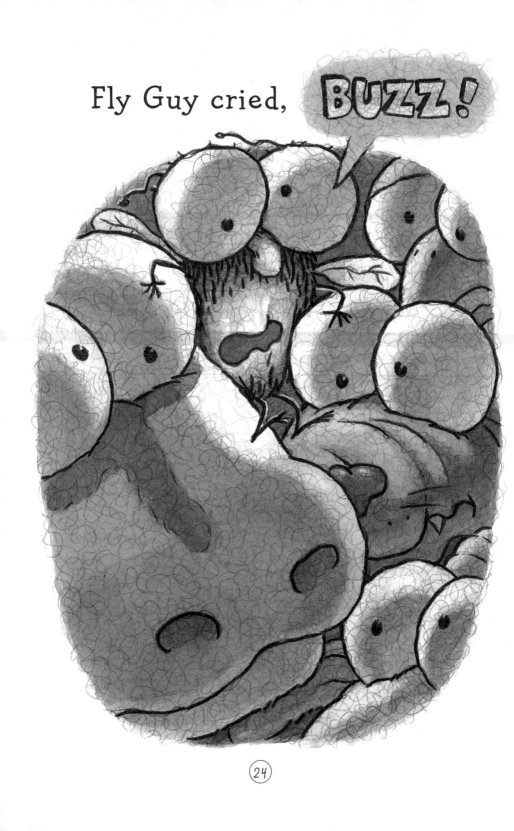

"I'm up here!" yelled Buzz.

Out came Fly Guy.

Out came the spider,
the bird, the cat, the dog,
the goat, and the cow.

And everyone lived
happily ever after,
of course!

FLY HIGH, FLY GUY!

Tedd Arnold

Cartwheel BOOKS ®

SCHOLASTIC INC.
New York   Toronto   London   Auckland
Sydney   Mexico City   New Delhi   Hong Kong

For Christene
—T.A.

Library of Congress Cataloging-in-Publication Data:
Arnold, Tedd.
Fly high, fly guy! / by Tedd Arnold.
  p. cm.
"Cartwheel books."
Summary: When Buzz, his parents, and his pet fly go on a road trip and get lost, Fly Guy comes to the rescue to help them find their way home.
ISBN 978-0-545-00722-1
[1. Flies--Fiction. 2. Automobile travel--Fiction.] I. Title.
PZ7.A7379Ro 2008
[E]—dc22   2007005317
                  ISBN 978-0-545-00722-1

10   11 12

Printed in Singapore 46
First printing, May 2008

A boy had a pet fly.
He named him Fly Guy.
Fly Guy could say
the boy's name—

Chapter 1

One day Buzz said,
"It's time to take
a road trip."

Fly Guy wanted to go, too.
"He's too little," said Mom.
"He might get lost."

"Sorry," said Dad.
"Fly Guy stays home."

He shut the trunk.
"Okay, let's hit the road!"

The family drove and drove.

They stopped for a picnic.
Mom opened the trunk.
Fly Guy flew out.

Dad said, "How did
he get in there?"

"Just don't lose him,"
said Mom and Dad.
"Now, let's eat!"

Chapter 2

They drove to the beach.

Then it was time to go.
Mom and Dad said,
"Is Fly Guy lost?"

"No," said Buzz.

"Here he is!"

They drove to
the art museum.

Then it was time to go.
Mom and Dad said,
"Is Fly Guy lost?"

"No," said Buzz.
"Here he is!"

They drove to
the fun park.

Then it was time to go.
Mom and Dad said,
"Is Fly Guy lost?"

"No," said Buzz.
"Here he is!"

Chapter 3

"It's time to go home,"
said Mom.
"Let's hit the road,"
said Dad.

They drove

and drove   and drove

and drove   and drove

and drove   and drove

and drove

and drove

and drove

and drove

and drove

and drove

But they did not get home.
"We're lost," said Mom
and Dad.

Buzz and Fly Guy had an idea.
Buzz said, "Fly high, Fly Guy!"

Fly Guy flew high into the sky.
He used his super fly eyes
to spy their house.

Fly Guy led the way home.

"Thank you, Fly Guy,"
said Mom and Dad.
"You saved the day!
Yay, Fly Guy!"

HOORAY FOR FLY GUY!

Tedd Arnold

SCHOLASTIC INC.

New York   Toronto   London   Auckland
Sydney   Mexico City   New Delhi   Hong Kong

For my alma mater, the University of Florida, and our great sports teams

GO, GATORS!

Copyright © 2008 by Tedd Arnold.

All rights reserved. Published by Scholastic Inc.
SCHOLASTIC, CARTWHEEL BOOKS, and associated logos
are trademarks and/or registered trademarks of Scholastic Inc.

No part of this publication may be reproduced, stored in a retrieval system, or transmitted
in any form or by any means, electronic, mechanical, photocopying, recording, or otherwise,
without written permission of the publisher. For information regarding permission, write to
Scholastic Inc., Attention: Permissions Department, 557 Broadway, New York, NY 10012.

Library of Congress Cataloging-in-Publication Data:

Arnold, Tedd.
  Hooray for Fly Guy! / Tedd Arnold.
    p. cm. -- (Fly Guy ; #6)
  "Cartwheel books."
  Summary: Fly Guy joins Buzz's football team, despite Coach's
  misgivings, and hits the field for a special, secret play.
  ISBN 978-0-545-00724-5
  [1. Flies--Fiction. 2. Football--Fiction.] I. Title.

  PZ7.A7379Hoo 2008
  [E]--dc22
                        2007037521

                ISBN 978-0-545-00724-5
10 9   11 12/0
                Printed in Singapore 46
                First printing, September 2008

A boy had a pet fly.
He named him Fly Guy.
Fly Guy could say
the boy's name—

Chapter 1

Fly Guy went with Buzz
to play football.

Coach said, "We need one more player for the big game."

Buzz said,
"Fly Guy can play."

Coach laughed.

"Flies can't play football."

Buzz said, "Fly Guy, show
him what you can do."
Fly Guy kicked the ball.

Fly Guy went out for a pass.

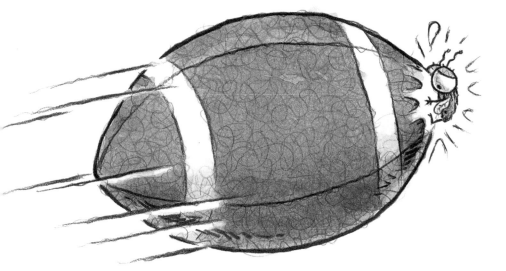

Fly Guy tried to tackle Buzz.

"I was right," said Coach.
"Flies can't play football.
But he can come to the
game."

Chapter 2

It was the day before the big game. Buzz made a helmet for Fly Guy.

They played football.

They did jumping jacks.

They planned a secret play.

They made up a
touchdown dance.

They went to the big game.
Coach said, "A new player
joined our team."

Fly Guy sat on the bench.

The game started.
His team scored.
Fly Guy cheered.

The other team scored.
Fly Guy worried.
The other team scored a lot!

Chapter 3

Finally, there was one
second left in the game.

The other team was ahead.
They were about to
score again.

And the new
player was hurt.

Coach said, "Okay, Fly Guy.
You can play now.
The game is lost anyway."

Buzz said, "It's time
for our secret play."

Fly Guy went to the line.

The other team snapped
the ball to their quarterback.

Fly Guy flew
fast and straight.

He flew right up the
quarterback's nose!

The boy dropped the ball.

Buzz picked it up and ran.

He scored!

Fly Guy and Buzz did their touchdown dance.

The team cheered. "We won!
Hooray for Fly Guy!"